Tiger Family Trip

Adapted by Becky Friedman
Based on the screenplay "Tiger Family Trip"
written by Becky Friedman and Jennifer Hamburg
Poses and layouts by Jason Fruchter

Simon Spotlight
New York   London   Toronto   Sydney   New Delhi

SIMON SPOTLIGHT
An imprint of Simon & Schuster Children's Publishing Division
1230 Avenue of the Americas, New York, New York 10020
This Simon Spotlight paperback edition March 2017
© 2017 The Fred Rogers Company
All rights reserved, including the right of reproduction in whole or in part in any form.
SIMON SPOTLIGHT and colophon are registered trademarks of Simon & Schuster, Inc.
For information about special discounts for bulk purchases, please contact Simon & Schuster
Special Sales at 1-866-506-1949 or business@simonandschuster.com.
Manufactured in the United States of America 0117 LAK
10 9 8 7 6 5 4 3 2 1
ISBN 978-1-4814-7745-1
ISBN 978-1-4814-7746-8 (eBook)

It was a big day for Daniel Tiger: His family was going on a trip to visit his grandfather.

"I'm going to give this to Grandpere. It's a picture of me and him. Our family trip is going to be grr-ific!"

Daniel and his family began to get ready for their trip!

Mom made snacks.

Dad packed up the suitcases.

Daniel packed his backpack with his favorite things.

"Trolley's here!" said Daniel.
At last the Tiger family was ready to go on their trip!

"What are we going to do on our trip?" Daniel asked.
"There are so many things to do and see when you're on a trip with your family," sang Mom. "I made a map of everything we're going to see on the way to Grandpere's. Let me show it to you."

"First we'll see the twisty road, then the dinosaur park with the big dinosaur slide, then the butterfly garden, and then Grandpere's house!"

"Wow! We're going to see all of these places?" asked Daniel.

"We sure are," said Mom.

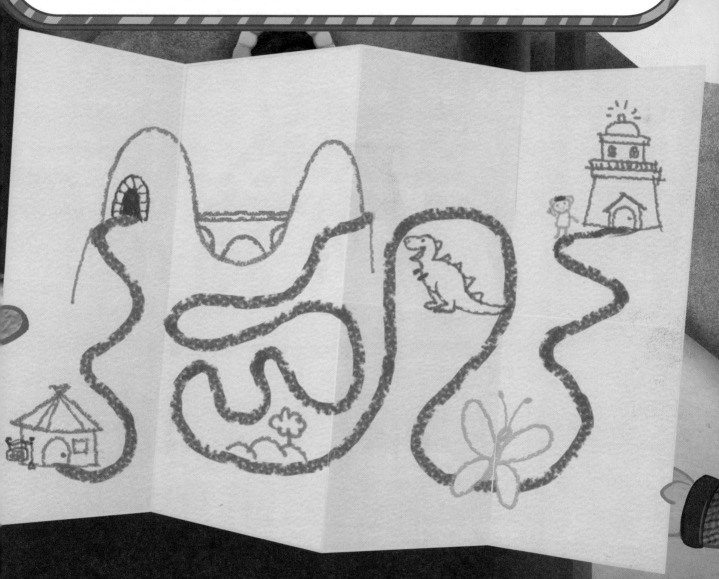

"Since we're seeing so many things on our trip, let's play Tiger Spy," Dad suggested.

"This Tiger spies . . . something green with big wheels!" said Daniel. Can you find what Daniel spies?

"This Tiger spies . . . something very twisty!" Mom smiled.

"It's the twisty road!" said Daniel excitedly. "That's the first thing on our map!"

There are so many things to do and see when you're on a trip with your family!

As Trolley rolled along the twisty road, Mom asked Daniel, "Daniel, your body is a little wiggly. Do you have to go potty?"

"Yes," said Daniel. "But where can I go potty?"

"There's a place to stop right here. You can go potty at the dinosaur playground," said Mom.

"I want to play on the dinosaur slide!" said Daniel as they got off Trolley.

"Daniel, *if you have to go potty, stop and go right away*," Mom reminded him.

"Okay," said Daniel. "I'll go potty . . . and *then* play on the dinosaur slide."

After Daniel went to the potty, he was ready to play!

"*STOMP! STOMP! STOMP!* I'm a BIG STOMPING dinosaur!" said Daniel. "Come on, Margaret. Let's go down the dinosaur slide together!"

"Wheeeee!" Margaret and Daniel giggled.

"It's time to get back on Trolley," Mom said a few minutes later. *"It's almost time to stop, so choose one more thing to do,"* Daniel sang. He chose to go down the dinosaur slide with Dad, and then it was time to go!

But when Daniel got back on Trolley, he didn't notice that he had left something behind.

"Are we there yet?" asked Daniel.

"Not yet," said Mom.

"It's very, very hard to wait," Daniel said with a sigh. He decided to play a game with Margaret.

"Where's your nose, Margaret?" Daniel asked. Margaret poked her nose . . . and then she poked Daniel! Daniel did not want to be poked. It made him *mad*.

"*When you feel so mad that you want to roar, take a deep breath and count to four*," sang Daniel. He felt calmer, and he gave Pandy to Margaret to play with.

Margaret smiled and stopped poking him.

Suddenly, Daniel saw one butterfly . . . and then another . . . and then another. "Look!" gasped Daniel. "It's the butterfly garden!" Daniel and his family got off Trolley to take a closer look.

There are so many things to do and see when you're on a trip with your family!

Daniel imagined that he and Margaret were playing with their butterfly friends.

After Daniel and his family got back on Trolley, Daniel was feeling a little squirmy again. "Are we there yet? Are we?" he asked.

"Daniel, I think there's only one place left on your map," said Mom. "Why don't you see what it is?"

Daniel pulled out the map. The last stop was . . .

Grandpere's house!

"Hello!" said Grandpere. "I am so happy to see you! How was your trip?"

"Tigertastic!" exclaimed Daniel. "We saw *so* many new things!"

"Grandpere!" said Daniel once they had settled in. "I brought a picture for you!"

But when Daniel reached into his bag . . . the picture was gone!

"I must have lost it," Daniel said. He was feeling very sad.

"I know you're sad about losing the picture," said Grandpere. "But maybe there's something else you can give me."

"Like what?" asked Daniel.

"Like a great big hug," said Grandpere, as he hugged Daniel. Daniel smiled. A hug did make him feel better.

"I made a special dinner for everyone outside," said Grandpere. Daniel and the whole Tiger family ate dinner under the stars.

After dinner it was time for bed. Daniel snuggled into his sleeping bag as Grandpere tucked him in.

"Good night, Daniel," said Grandpere.

"Good night, Grandpere."

I had a grr-ific time on our Tiger family trip today. We saw so many new things together. I'm glad you could come too. Ugga Mugga!